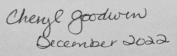

Also by Beth Bacon

I Hate Reading

# THE BOOK NO ONE WANTS TO READ

by Beth Bacon

**HARPER**

*An Imprint of HarperCollinsPublishers*

Library of Congress Control Number: 2020947244

ISBN 978-0-06-296254-6

21 22 23 24 25   EP   10 9 8 7 6 5 4 3 2 1

❖

Originally published in 2017 by Pixel Titles.

To the students and staff
at Miramar Ranch Elementary

How about that!
You picked me up!

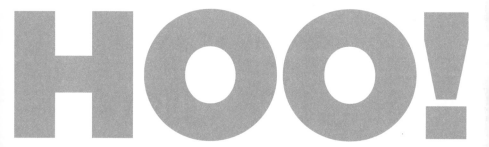

# HOO!

Someone actually
wants to read me.

I've been waiting for ages for someone like you to choose me.

Are you ready to get started?

# Wait—*what?*

**WHY
ARE YOU
LOOKING
AT ME LIKE
THAT?**

I'VE SEEN
THAT LOOK
BEFORE.

You're not one of those kids who thinks books are boring, are you?

# OH.
# I GET IT.

You only picked me up
because you had to.

# YOU'D RATHER BE

---▶ ✖

# SOMEWHERE ELSE

✖ ◀---

# ANYWHERE ELSE

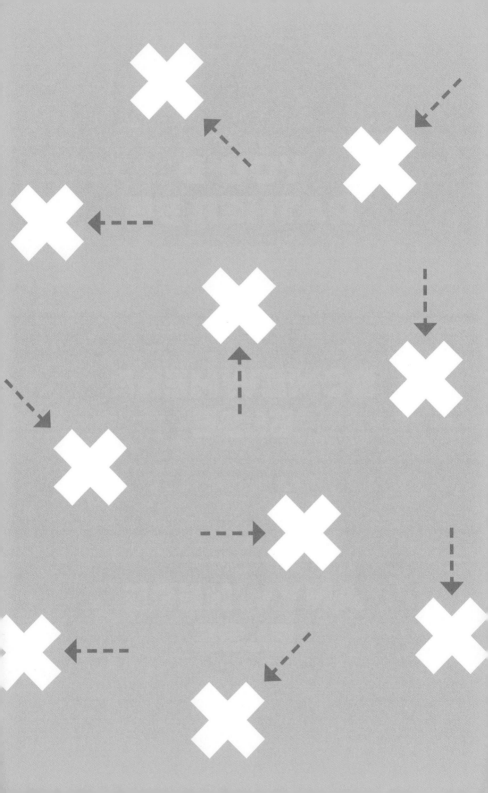

# EVERYWHERE ELSE.

If you think reading is boring, try sitting around all day facing the wall, cover closed, doing a whole lot of *nothing*.

Hey,
I might
have an idea
that helps us
both.

# WHAT IF...

# YOU

sit here and turn
my pages, and…

# WE

just goof off?

Everyone will think
you're reading.

And I get a little time
off the shelf.

# I WON'T TELL ANYONE
## IF YOU WON'T.

# Are you in?

# Let's shake on it.

# WAIT, I DON'T HAVE HANDS.

# Well, just

me anyway.

Yeah! That's what I'm talking about.

LET'S
GET
PAID
STARTED

# Do you like scratch and sniff?

# SCRATCH HERE.

Smells like paper, huh?

# Now try this:

SCRATCH
HERE.

Stinky, right?

# GOTCHA!

Still paper.

I'm just having
a little fun.

Give me
another chance.

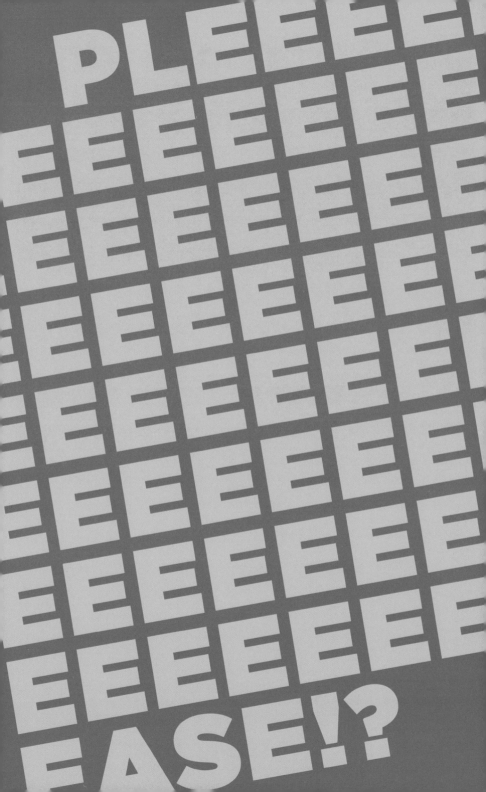

Let's play my
favorite game.

# ROCK

# PAPER

# SCISSORS

# We each think of one of these things:

**ROCK**

**PAPER**

**SCISSORS**

When I say,

"GO,"

we both say what
we're thinking.

Here's how we tell
who wins:

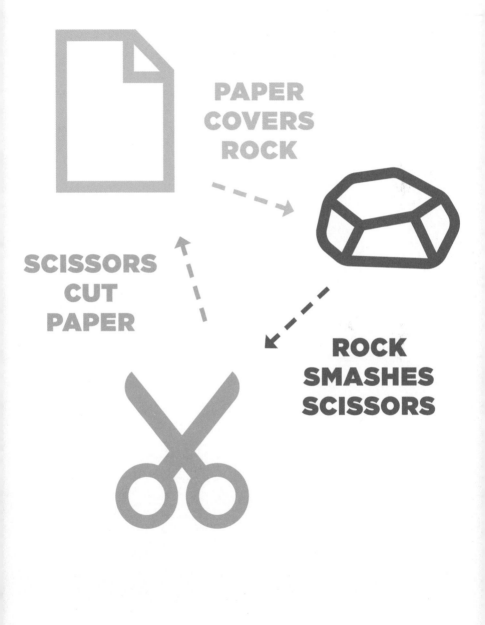

Did I win? HA!
Let's try again.

# GOTCHA!

Wait, you got me?

Can you read
my mind?

Nevermind.

Wow, you won again?
You're too good!

Let's try
something else.

# BLINK.

How about

# BLINK.

a staring contest.

# BLINK.

Those are fun.

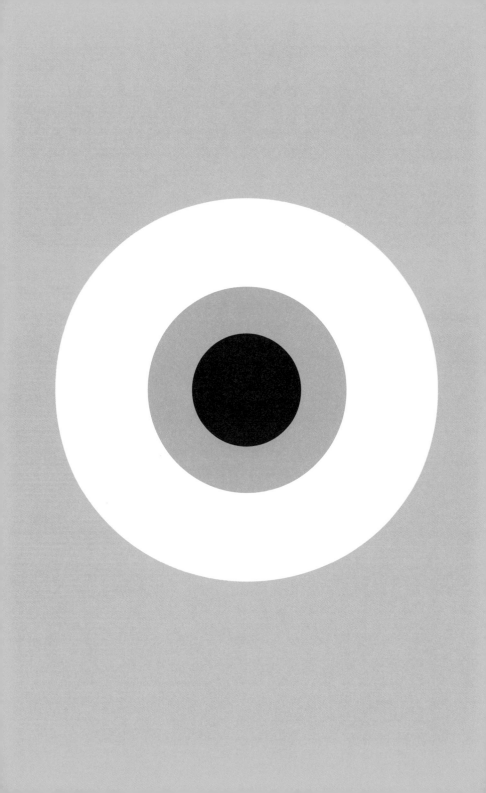

You blinked!

(I don't have eyelids.)

Speaking of
eyelids, can you

WINK?

Close one eye.

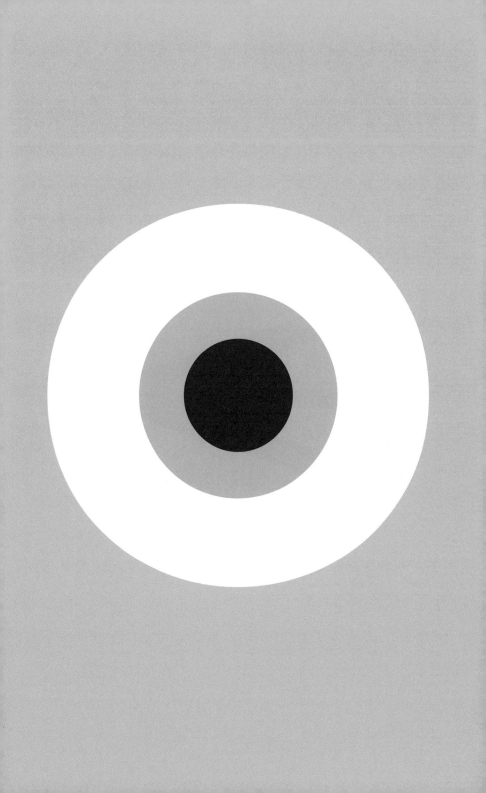

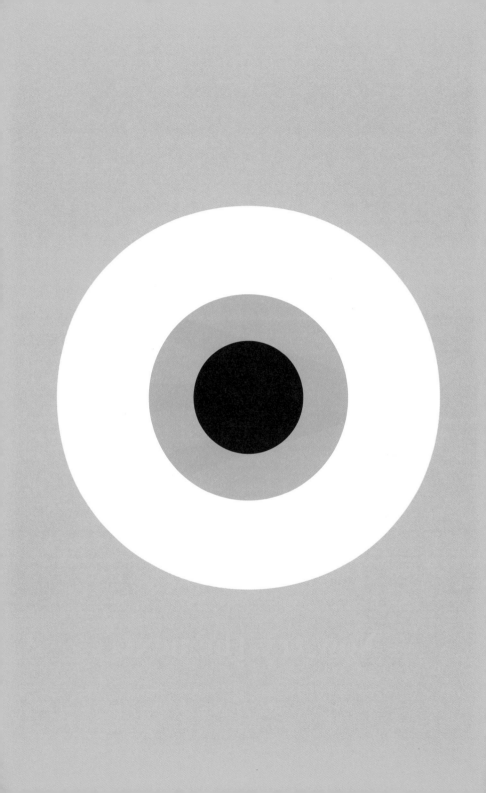

Now try the next.

Why is one side

harder than the other?

Careful—don't close
both at the same time.

(Someone might think
you're not reading.)

Some kids can roll their tongue like a taco.

Can you?

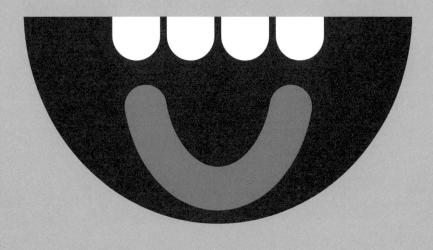

What about
wiggling
your ears?

# Then try wiggling

your nose instead!

Now wiggle your butt.

# But not too much!

(People will definitely think you're not reading.)

# Try wiggling your ears

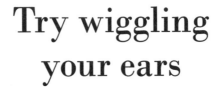

nose and butt
all together.

Now
wink

and
make a
tongue taco!

# UH-OH!

Is someone looking?

# QUICK!

Turn the page.

ing, reading, reading, reading, reading, readin
reading, reading, reading, reading, reading, re
ing, reading, reading, reading, reading, readin
reading, reading, reading, reading, reading, re
ing, reading, reading, reading, reading, readin
reading, reading, reading, reading, reading, re
ing, reading, reading, reading, reading, readin
reading, reading, reading, reading, reading, re
ing, reading, reading, reading, reading, readin
read                                    ing, re
ing,    **PRETEND YOU'RE** readin
read         **READING.**              ing, re
ing,                                    readin
reading, reading, reading, reading, reading, re
ing, reading, reading, reading, reading, readin
reading, reading, reading, reading, reading, re
ing, reading, reading, reading, reading, readin
reading, reading, reading, needing, reading, re
ing, reading, reading, reading, reading, readin
reading, reading, reading, reading, reading, re
ing, reading, reading, reading, reading, readin
reading, reading, reading, reading, reading, re
ing, needing, reading, reading, reading, readin
reading, reading, reading, reading, reading, re
ing, reading, reading, reading, reading, readin
reading, reading, reading, reading, reading, re
ing, reading, reading, reading, reading, readin

reading, reading, reading, reading, reading, reading,
ing, reading, reading, reading, reading, reading,
reading, reading, reading, reading, reading, reading,
ing, reading, reading, reading, reading, reading,
reading, reading, reading, reading, reading, reading,
ing, reading, reading, reading, reading, reading,
reading, reading, reading, reading, reading, reading,
ing, reading, needing, reading, reading, reading,
reading, reading, reading, reading, reading, reading,
ing, reading, reading, reading, reading, reading,
reading, reading, reading, reading, reading, reading,
ing, reading, reading, reading, reading, reading,
reading, reading, reading, reading, reading, reading,
ing, reading, reading, reading, reading, reading,
reading,              **SQUINT. NOD.**              ing, re
ing, read            **TILT YOUR**                 reading,
reading,                **HEAD.**                   ing, re
ing, read                                           readin,
reading, reading, reading, reading, reading, reading,
ing, reading, reading, reading, reading, reading,
reading, reading, reading, reading, reading, reading,
ing, reading, reading, reading, reading, reading,
reading, reading, reading, reading, reading, reading,
ing, reading, reading, reading, reading, reading,
reading, reading, reading, reading, reading, reading,
ing, reading, reading, reading, reading, reading,
reading, reading, reading, reading, reading, reading,

You might want to bookmark that last page so you can flip there whenever someone checks to see if you're reading.

**IT'S SURE TO FOOL THEM.**

Oh, and some of the words back there don't say "reading." Bet you can't find them.

Let me know if you are **NEEDING** help.

(Psst. There are three.)

Follow the maze
to the ✖ with
your finger.

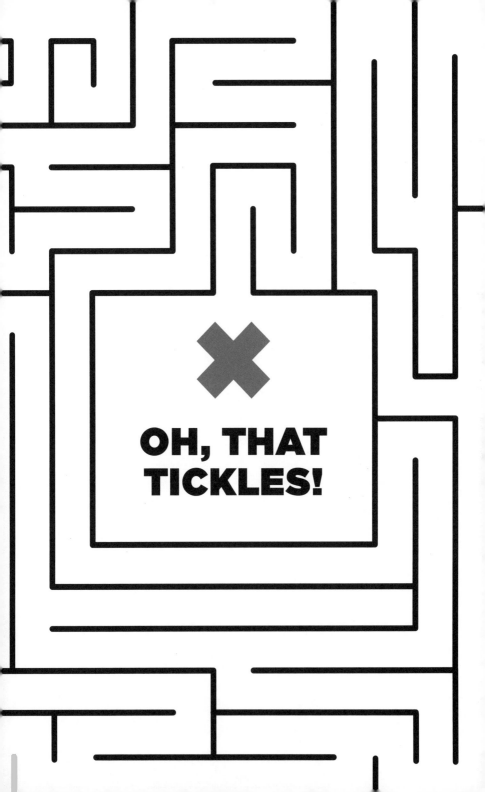

OH, THAT TICKLES!

What do mazes have
to do with reading?

**NOTHING!**

But when some kids read, they drag their finger under the sentence.

It's like they have
an eye at the end
of their finger.

# WHAT IF THEY DID?

Every time they point,
they'd poke themselves in the eye!

OUCH!

Hey, I have a joke.

Want to hear it?

What's the tallest building in the world?

A library, because it has so many stories!

Not funny? Geez. Tough crowd.

Here's another.

Did you hear about
the anti-gravity book?

That one's my favorite.

Do you think it's about me?

I *can* call you friend
now, right?

Friends help each
other out, and that's
what we're doing.

# IT SURE FEELS GOOD TO HAVE A FRIEND!

Do you like puzzlers?
I do. Here's one:

Try to get the red
glass off the tray.

Stumped?
Flip me upside
down!

Flip me
again!

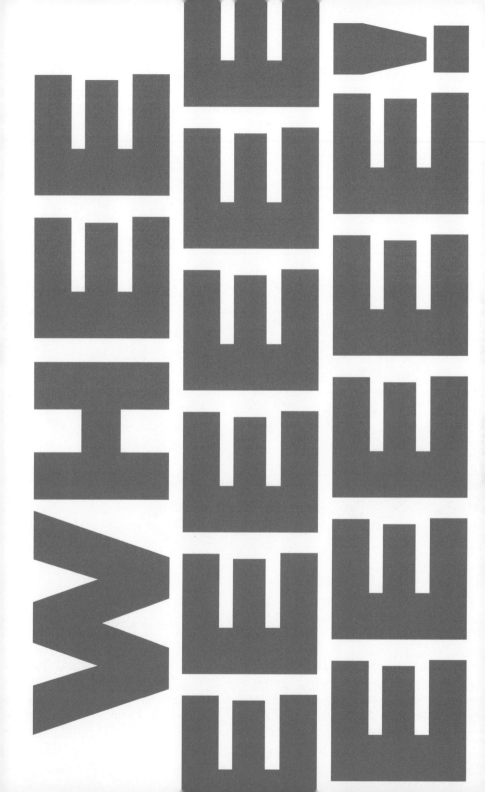

WHEEEEEEEEEEEEEY!

AGAIN! AND AGAIN!

AND... W

Just give me a
minute

till everything
stops spinning.

Just pretend
you're reading.

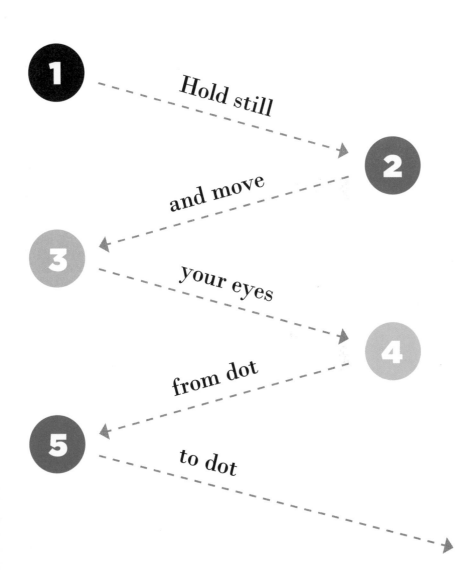

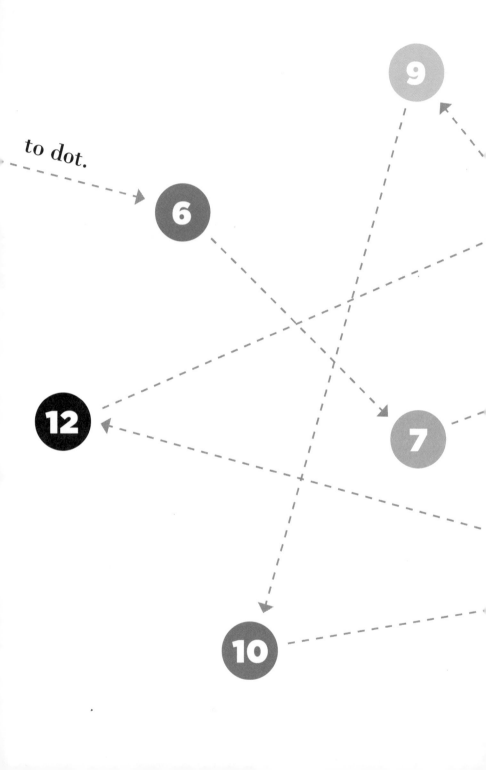

**13**

**8**

**11**

Sorry. Sometimes I get a little crazy. Let's move on.

# What do these

# three phrases have

# in common?

# TACO CAT

# YO BANANA BOY

# TOO BAD I HID A BOOT

Each one is spelled

the same backward

as forward.

TACO CAT

YO BANANA BOY

TOO BAD I HID A BOOT

(Even in a mirror.)

Which **BLUE LINE** is longer?

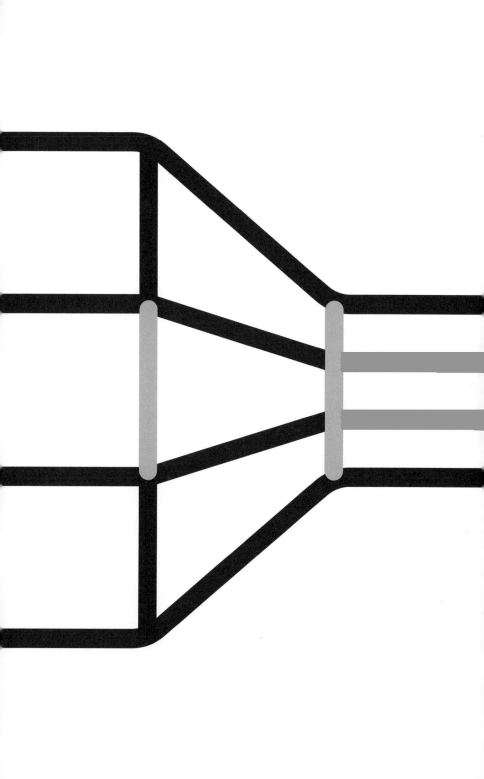

Tricked you.
They're the same.

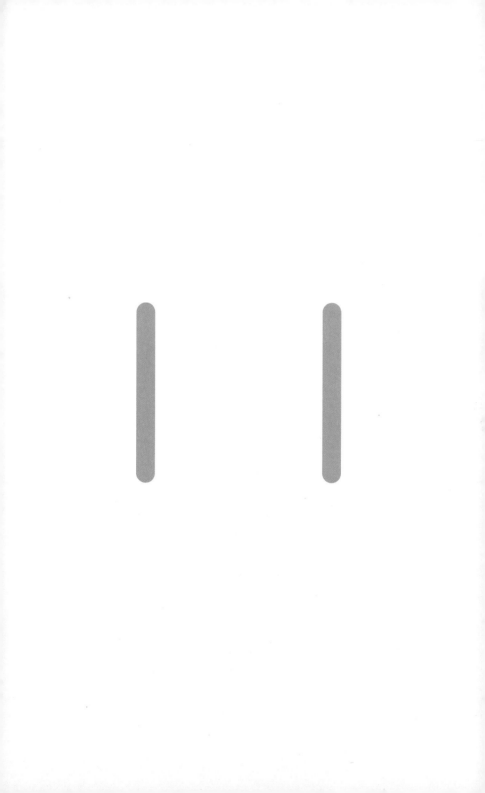

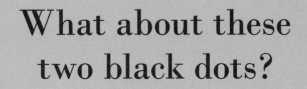

What about these
two black dots?

Which one is
bigger?

Yup.

Same, same.

# What if I told you

these lines are the same
length too?

# You got me.

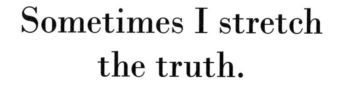

Sometimes I stretch
the truth.

Speaking of
stretching, my
spine could use
a little

Now that was
relaxing.

YAWN.

You're not yawning too,
are you?

Wow, it looks like I'm coming to an end.

# I HAD A BLAST!

Anytime you want to hang out, I'll be right where you left me.

HMM...

You look kinda
bummed out.

Not *that* kind of bum.

*(Sheesh.)*

Don't worry about me. I'll feel good going back on the shelf knowing I have a pal.

If you don't want to
stop, you can always
go back to page

OK.

Oh, I forgot again.
I don't have hands, so

# JUST SMACK ME HERE.

Just kidding!
(Didn't hurt.)